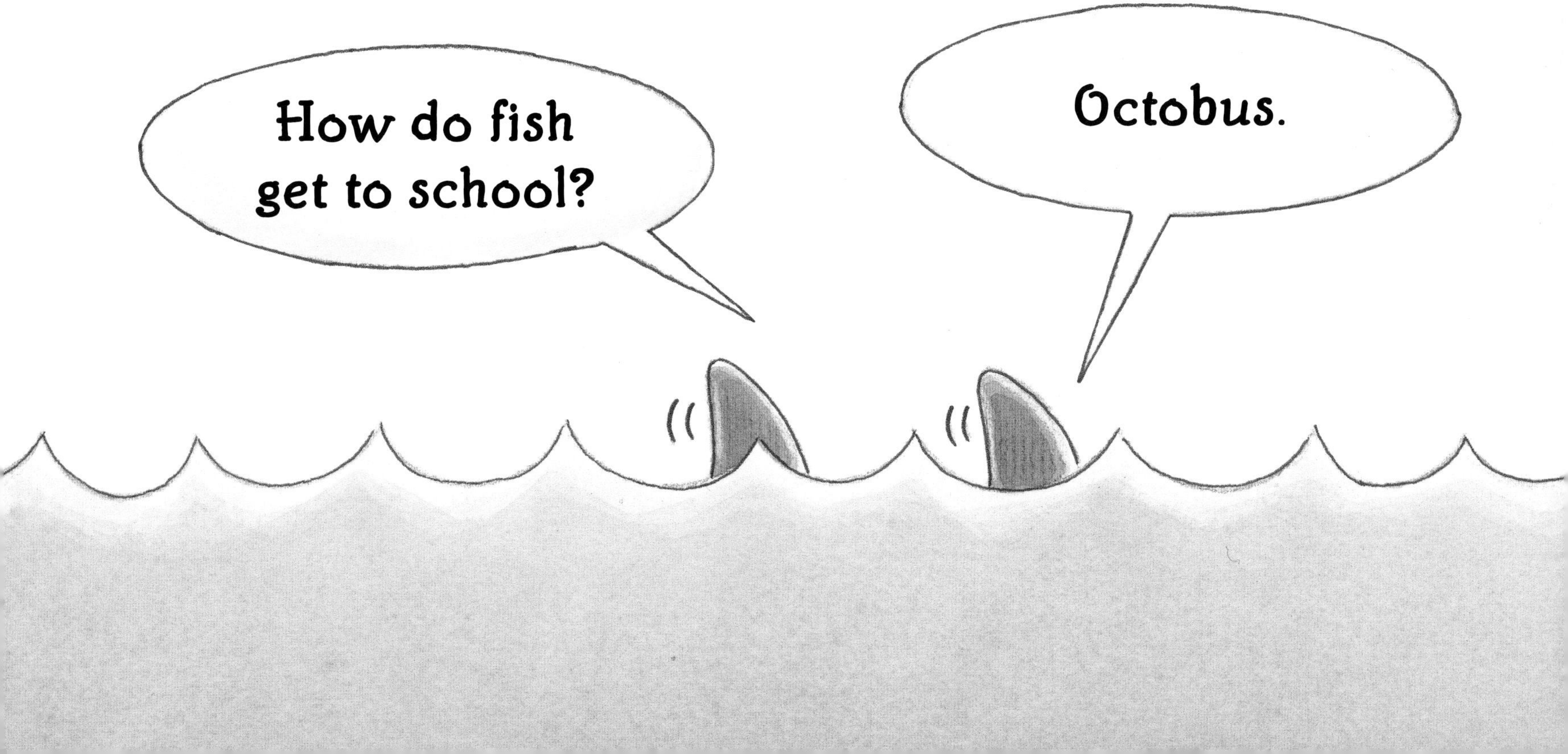
How do fish get to school?
Octobus.

To James Fraser, with thanks for his help with the jokes!
—T. G.

For William, another book for you to *dive* into
—N. N.

Flip & Fin: We Rule the School!
Copyright © 2014 by HarperCollins Publishers
All rights reserved. Manufactured in China. For information address HarperCollins Children's Books,
a division of HarperCollins Publishers, 10 East 53rd Street, New York, NY 10022.
www.harpercollinschildrens.com

Watercolors were used to prepare the full-color art.
The text type is 30-point Beton T Bold.

Library of Congress Cataloging-in-Publication Data

Gill, Timothy, (date)
Flip & Fin : we rule the school! / by Timothy Gill ; illustrated by Neil Numberman.
pages cm
Summary: Flip, a sand shark, practices all week for Joke Day at school, but when the time comes
and he faces a big crowd, Flip freezes until his twin brother, Fin, comes to the rescue.
ISBN 978-0-06-224300-3 (trade ed.)
[1. Jokes—Fiction. 2. Stage fright—Fiction. 3. Twins—Fiction. 4. Brothers—Fiction.
5. Schools—Fiction. 6. Sand tiger shark—Fiction.] I. Numberman, Neil, illustrator.
II. Title. III. Title: We rule the school!
PZ7.G3995Fli 2014 [E]—dc23 2013030044

14 15 16 17 18 SCP 10 9 8 7 6 5 4 3 2 1
First Edition
Greenwillow Books

Flip & Fin

We Rule the School!

BY

Timothy Gill

ILLUSTRATED BY

Neil Numberman

Greenwillow Books
An Imprint of HarperCollins Publishers

This is Flip.

This is Fin.

Flip and Fin,
the sand shark twins.

"Hey, Fin," said Flip on the way to school.

"Joke Day is coming up. And I've got a good one.

What did the sawfish see?"

"I don't know, Flip," said Fin.

"He saw fish!" said Flip.

Ugh.

"That's bad," said Fin.

"Is not," said Flip.

"Is too," said Fin. "Yup. Pretty bad. You need more practice."

At recess, Fin built a sand castle with Swimmy.

Flip told jokes to anyone who would listen.

"Knock, knock," he said to Molly.

"Who's there?" said Molly.

"Orange," said Flip.

"Orange who?" said Molly.

"Orange . . . orange . . . oh, I forget," said Flip.

Molly snorted. "Lucky for you,

Joke Day is not today," she said.

Fin pulled Flip to
the pirate's chest.
"Ahoy!" yelled Fin. "I call blue!"
"Avast!" yelled Flip. "I call yellow!"
"Super Sharks!" yelled Flip and Fin.
"We rule the school!"

"Hey, Fin," said Flip.

"What did the octopus say to his girlfriend?"

"I give up," said Fin.

"I wanna hold your hand, hand, hand, hand, hand, hand, hand, hand."

"Ha-ha!" said Fin. "Pretty good, Flipster."

"Yup," yelled Flip. "I'm a Super Shark!"

The next day, Flip woke up bright and early.

He brushed his teeth. He had a lot of teeth.

It took a long time.

He looked in the mirror.

"What side of a fish has the most scales?" he said to the mirror.

"The outside! Ha-ha."

Flip laughed. Toothpaste dribbled down his chin.

"Pretty chomping good!"

At school, Flip and Fin learned about
the letters J and A and W and S.
They drew pictures for their mom and dad.
The bell rang. It was recess.

Jetty
Jellyfish
Jolly Roger
Jonah
Jetsam

"Hey, Swimmy," said Flip.

"What did the sardine call the submarine?"

"Beats me," said Swimmy. "What?"

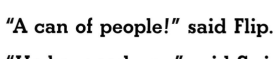

"A can of people!" said Flip.

"Ha-ha, good one," said Swimmy.

"Yup," agreed Molly.

"You can tell that joke on Joke Day, for sure."

"Listen up, guys!" said Flip.

"What lies at the bottom of the sea and shakes?"

"I dunno," said Molly. "What?"

"What?" said Swimmy.

"What?" said Fin, looking up from his sand castle.

"A nervous wreck," said Flip.

"Ha-ha!" said Swimmy. "Excellento, Flipster."

"Do you think anyone will laugh?" asked Flip.

"Yup," said Molly.

"For sure!" said Fin.

Flip kept practicing his jokes.

"What's the difference between a fish and a piano?

You can't tuna fish!"

"Wow," said Fin. "You know a lot of funny jokes, Flippy-dippy."

"But now I can't decide which one to tell," said Flip.

"Hey, Flip," said Fin. "Who rules the school?"

SUPER SHARKS!

Finally, it was Joke Day.

Flip listened as the big kids told their jokes.

"Knock, knock," said Rocko Swordfish.

"Who's there?" everybody said.

"Ira," said Rocko.

"Ira who?" everybody replied.

"Ira-member you, why don't you remember me?" said Rocko.

Everybody clapped and cheered.

Which joke should Flip tell?

He still couldn't decide.

Plus, he would have to stand in front of

everyone in his school

and speak into a microphone.

He had forgotten to plan for that.

Onstage, Celia Starfish stood and stared at the audience.

Then she turned around.

Her arms quivered, but her voice was loud and clear.

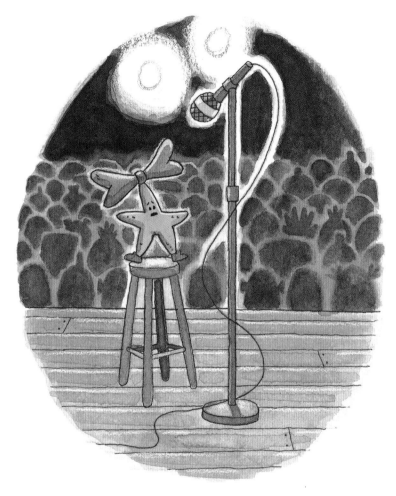

"Knock, knock," she said.

"Who's there?" everyone answered.

"Orange," said Celia.

"Orange who?"

"Orange you glad I didn't say banana?" Celia said.

The crowd went wild!

Finally it was Flip's turn.

"You can do it," whispered Fin.

The stage was big and high.

Flip cleared his throat.

Dozens of eyes stared up at him.

Flip stared back.

He smiled his best smile.

A little bead of sweat trickled down his nose.

"Er, er. . . ." He stammered,

but no other sound came out.

"Hey, Flip!" yelled Fin.

"What kind of fish do you put in a peanut butter sandwich?"

Flip looked up. There was Fin.

And Molly. And Swimmy. And Mom and Dad, too.

"Jellyfish!" said Flip. He said it right into the microphone.

Everyone laughed.

"Hey, Fin," yelled Flip.

"What did one tide pool say to the other?"

"Show me your mussels!" said Fin.

Even the big kids were laughing now!

Did you know . . .

Sand sharks like Flip and Fin look very scary, because they have teeth that go every which way and stick out (even with their mouths closed), but they are usually not aggressive . . . unless you are a small fish, since that is what sand sharks eat! Sand sharks can come to the surface of the water and gulp air, then store it in their stomachs to help them float.

Anglerfish like Molly lure their prey with a rod that juts out above their mouths and glows. Millions of bioluminescent bacteria (that means bacteria that glow!) make the light. Anglerfish have jaws so big, they can swallow other fish up to two times their size.

Jellyfish like Swimmy don't have hearts or lungs or brains or bones or lots of other organs, but they do have a stomach and a mouth! They use their mouths both to eat and to release waste. Many jellyfish have tentacles full of toxins, and they use them to sting and catch their prey.

Starfish like Celia don't have any blood! Instead, filtered sea water pumps through their bodies to give them nutrients.

Swordfish like Rocko have "brain heaters," special tissues near their eyes that use their blood to keep their eyes and brains warm, even in cold water. That helps them see their prey better.